Before reading

Look at the book cov
Ask, "What do you th

To build independen   ed
at the start of this b   )
back to pages 6 and 7 in su a...
the child.

During reading

Offer plenty of support and praise as the child reads the story.
Listen carefully and respond to events in the text.

In 5c, the new **Key Words** are not shown at the bottom of
the page. If the child hesitates over a word, turn to the back
of the book to practise reading it together. If the word is
phonically decodable, you can sound out the letters and
blend the sounds to read the word ("d-o-g, dog"). Praise the
child for their effort, then return to the story.

Pause every few pages and ask questions to check the child's
understanding of what they have read. If they begin to lose
concentration, stop reading and save the page for later.

Celebrate the child's achievement and come back to the
story the next day.

After reading

After reading this book, ask, "Did you enjoy the story? What did
you like about it?" Encourage the child to share their opinions.

Use the comprehension questions on page 54 to check the
child's understanding and recall of the text.

Ladybird

Series Consultant: Professor David Waugh
With thanks to Kulwinder Maude

LADYBIRD BOOKS

UK | USA | Canada | Ireland | Australia
India | New Zealand | South Africa

Ladybird Books is part of the Penguin Random House group of companies
whose addresses can be found at global.penguinrandomhouse.com.
www.penguin.co.uk   www.puffin.co.uk   www.ladybird.co.uk

Penguin
Random House
UK

Original edition of Key Words with Peter and Jane first published by Ladybird Books Ltd 1964
Series updated 2023
This book first published 2023
001

Text copyright © Ladybird Books Ltd, 1964, 2023
Illustrations by Flora Aranyi
Based on characters and design by Gustavo Mazali
Illustrations copyright © Ladybird Books Ltd, 2023

With thanks to Liz Pemberton for her contributions in advising on the illustrations
With thanks to Inclusive Minds for connecting us with their Inclusion Ambassador network,
and in particular thanks to Guntaas Kaur Chugh for her input on the illustrations

Printed in China

The authorized representative in the EEA is Penguin Random House Ireland,
Morrison Chambers, 32 Nassau Street, Dublin D02 YH68

A CIP catalogue record for this book is available from the British Library

ISBN: 978-0-241-51087-2

All correspondence to:
Ladybird Books
Penguin Random House Children's
One Embassy Gardens, 8 Viaduct Gardens, London SW11 7BW

MIX
Paper from
responsible sources
FSC® C018179
FSC
www.fsc.org

Key Words

with Peter and Jane

5c

Granny and Grandad

Based on the original
Key Words with Peter and Jane
reading scheme and research by William Murray

Original edition written by William Murray
This edition written by Chitra Soundar
Illustrated by Flora Aranyi
Based on characters and design by Gustavo Mazali

Peter and Jane are at Granny and Grandad's home.

There is Grandad. There is Granny. There is Max, Grandad's little dog.

There are fun things to do at Granny and Grandad's.

"What will we do with Granny and Grandad?" Jane says to Peter.

"Let's go to the little pond," says Peter.

"Yes, we will go there," says Grandad.

Peter and Grandad see frogs in the little pond.

"Let's go to the fruit trees," says Grandad.

"Let's pick some fruit," says Peter.

Peter likes working with Grandad.

Jane likes working with Granny.

"Can you put that little dish there?" says Granny.

Jane puts the little dish there for her.

"Thanks," says Granny.

13

"We have some fruit for you," says Grandad. "Peter will put some there."

"Thanks," says Granny.

"Can I work with you, Granny?" Peter says.

"There is a big pan in there," says Granny.

"I will get it," says Jane.

"That *is* a big pan!" Peter says.

Jane gets the big pan.

"Thanks," says Granny.

17

"This is my cat, Ben," says Jane. She tells Grandad what things her little cat likes to do.

Peter tells Granny what his little rabbits like to play with.

Granny and Grandad do not have cats and rabbits.

"What do cats do, Jane?"
says Granny.

"My cat naps," says Jane.

"What do rabbits do,
Peter?" says Grandad.

"My rabbits hop,"
says Peter.

"Animals do things like
that," says Grandad.

Max is digging for things.

Peter and Jane are running to Max.

"Do not dig," says Peter.

"Animals do things like that," says Grandad. "Let him dig there."

"Let's go to the big pond," says Grandad. "We will see animals there."

"Look, Peter, there is an animal," says Jane.

"That is a big horse," says Peter.

"Do you want to give the horses some fruit?" says Granny.

Peter lets the big horse have some fruit.

Jane lets the little horse have some fruit.

"There is the big pond!"
says Peter.

"Look!" says Jane. "There
is a big cat."

"What is an animal like
that doing here?"
says Peter.

The big cat hops off the rocks and jumps near Peter.

The cat wants to be near Peter.

"I like this cat," says Peter.

Max looks at the cat.

"There are fish in the pond," says Granny.

"They are little fish," says Jane.

"There are big fish in the pond at Pippa's farm," says Peter.

There are big boats and little boats on the pond.

"Look at the boats zooming on the pond!" says Peter. "I want to do that."

"Let's go home and get some tea," says Grandad.

"Yes! Will you let me play with Max at home?"
says Peter.

Granny and Grandad say yes.

37

"There is a big horse," says Granny.

"And there is a little horse," says Jane.

"My friend Pippa has a little horse. I like to pat him," says Peter.

"There is Granny and Grandad's home," says Peter.

"Will there be good things for tea?" Jane says.

"Will there be jam tarts?" Peter says. "I want a big one!"

There are big trees at Granny and Grandad's home.

Grandad puts a rug near a tree. Granny puts things on the rug.

Grandad lets Max sit with him.

"Thanks for the tea, Granny," says Jane.

"Thank you," says Peter.

"I can see a big tin in there!" Jane says. "Will there be a treat in it?"

Granny has her big tin.

"Will there be jam tarts in there?" says Peter.

"What is in the tin, Granny?" says Jane.

"My jam tarts!" says Granny.

47

"A little one for her, and a little one for him," says Granny.

"I want a big jam tart, Granny!" Peter says.

Max barks.

"Jam tarts are not for you, Max," says Grandad.

Peter gets Max his tea.

Jane gives him some water.

Max barks.

"He is saying thanks," says Grandad.

"Good boy, Max," says Granny.

51

Mum is here.

Peter and Jane hug
Granny, Grandad
and Max.

"Thanks, Granny. Thanks,
Grandad," they say.

"Let's go home,"
says Mum.

Off they go!

Questions

Answer these questions about
the story.

1 What work does Peter do with
Grandad?

2 What do the children see zooming
on the pond?

3 What does Peter want for tea?

4 Why does Max the dog bark at the
end of the story?